¡VAMOS!

Let's Go to the Market

gallo

sol

by **Raúl the Third**

Colors by **Elaine Bay**

techo

VERSIFY
HOUGHTON MIFFLIN HARCOURT
BOSTON NEW YORK

*To Arielle Eckstut for inviting me to begin this journey
and to mi prima Annette Torres for taking amazing photos of
my inspiration, El Mercado Cuauhtémoc in Juárez.
—Raúl*

*To my mom for teaching me how to color.
—Elaine*

All rights reserved. For information about permission to reproduce selections from this
book, write to trade.permissions@hmhco.com or to Permissions, Houghton Mifflin
Harcourt Publishing Company, 3 Park Avenue, 19th Floor, New York, New York 10016.

hmhco.com

The illustrations in this book were done in ink on smooth plate
Bristol board with Adobe Photoshop for color.
The text type was set in Stempel Garamond LT Std.
The display type was set in Latin MT Std.
Hand lettering by Raúl Gonzalez

Library of Congress Cataloging-in-Publication Data is on file.
ISBN: 978-1-328-55726-1

Manufactured in China
SCP 10 9 8 7 6 5 4 3 2 1
4500744791

¡VAMOS! LET'S GO!

For breakfast Little Lobo and Bernabé eat huevos rancheros con tortillas de maíz and wash it down with warm milk.

Everywhere people are going to work. Everyone has a different job.

Next to the Mercado is La Placita.
There are many things to see and do.

Little Lobo and Bernabé make their way through the crowd. Everyone is busy!

Mal Burro and Peeky Pequeño keep La Placita and the Mercado clean. La viejita de la fuente feeds the pigeons.

placita

puesto

PEPINOS

ENSALADAS DE FRUTA

EDIFICIO

TORO

FUERTE

hombre fuerte

Little Lobo stops to watch the dancers perform.

Lobo delivery

bailador folklórico

The Mercado is a maze of pathways, shops, and booths.

Little Lobo's first delivery is at Chiva's Zonkey. There is a long line of tourists waiting to get their pictures taken.

Chiva draws stripes on the donkey with the shoe polish and turns it into a zonkey!

In the next shop, Señora Amparo sells herbs, medicines, and candles.

At their booth, Mr. and Mrs. Praderas sell sombreros for every occasion. Little Lobo bought his hat there.

Señor Duende sells books, magazines, newspapers, and Little Lobo's favorite . . . comic books!

I brought you your clothespins, Búho.

pinzas para la ropa

At their booth, Beto and Cuca sell desert plants and build small houses for every occasion.

Piñatas Caminos

PALO

TORO DULCE

Beep Boop!

tijeras

MONSTRUO

LA RUTA

Next, Little Lobo delivers the tissue paper Corrina Caminos needs to finish her piñatas. She's working on a piñata of the local legend El Toro!

She uses different colors of tissue paper to bring her creations to life and tijeras to create frilly textures.

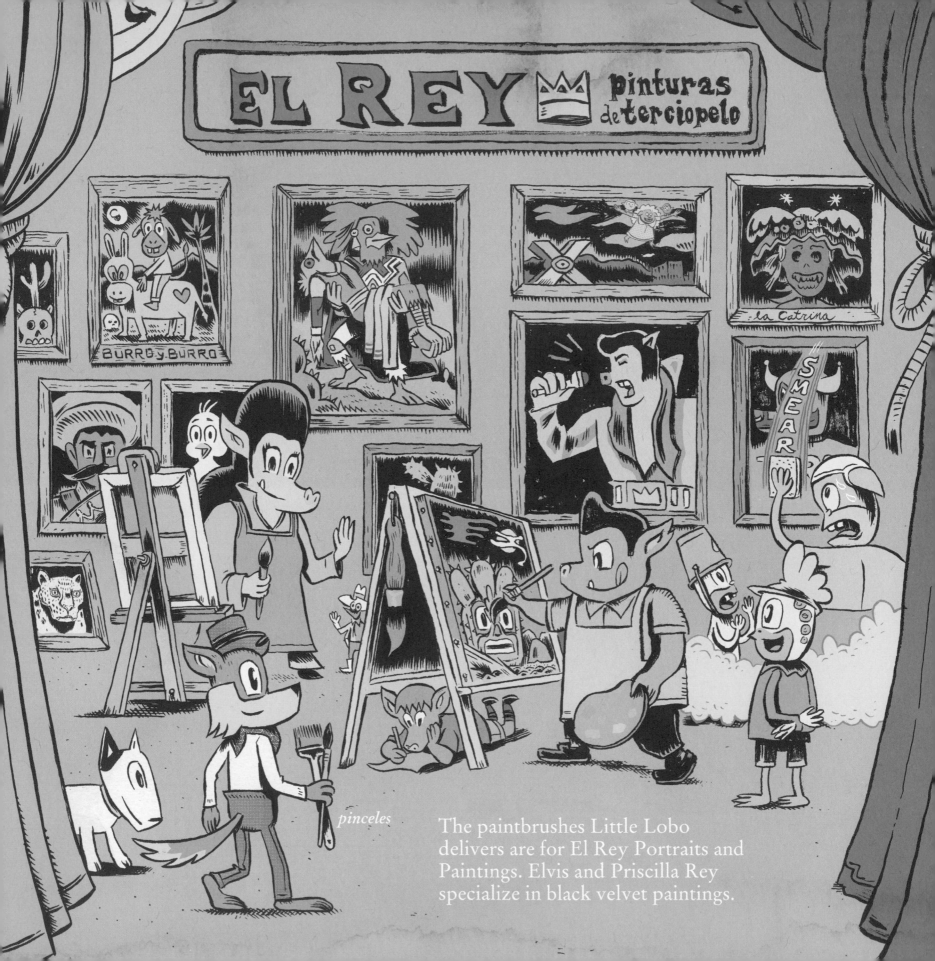

EL REY 👑 pinturas de terciopelo

BURRO y BURRO

la Catrina

SMEAR

pinceles

The paintbrushes Little Lobo delivers are for El Rey Portraits and Paintings. Elvis and Priscilla Rey specialize in black velvet paintings.

Good to see you, Little Lobo. Here is the portrait I owe you.

retrato

Checking his wagon, Little Lobo sees that he has collected as many things as he has delivered. He has only one item left to deliver. The Golden Laces, los Cordones de Oro.

pata

pintura

Little Lobo saved his favorite shop for last!
Masks, posters, and toys remind Little Lobo
of his favorite wrestler.

LUCHA LIBRE

CHAMP

la OINKOINK

TORO

LUCHA

BOW

el BOW WOW

juguetes

Little Lobo is happy
to give his hero a ride.

GLOSSARY*

*These are only some of the words found in Little Lobo's story. Be sure to look up other ones you don't know in a Spanish/English dictionary!

(La) **Acera** – Sidewalk
(El) **Agua** – Water
(La) **Alcancía** – Piggy bank
(Los) **Artistas callejeros** – Street performers
(El) **Autobús** – Bus
(El) **Bailador folklórico** – Folk dancer
(El) **Barril** – Barrel
(El) **Barro** – Clay
(La) **Bolera** – Shoeshine woman
(El) **Búho** – Owl
(El) **Burro** – Donkey
(El) **Buzón** – Mailbox
(La) **Cachucha** – Cap
(La) **Caja** – Cash register
(Las) **Cajas** – Boxes
(La) **Calle** – Street
(La) **Cama** – Bed
(Las) **Canicas** – Marbles
(El) **Carrito** – Wagon
(La) **Casa** – House
(Las) **Casitas** – Small houses
(Las) **Chanclas** – Flip-flops
(El) **Chicle** – Chewing gum
(Los) **Cordones de oro** – Golden laces
(La) **Crema de zapatos** – Shoe polish
(El) **Cuarto** – Bedroom
(El) **Desayuno** – Breakfast
(El) **Desierto** – Desert
(La) **Despensa** – Storage room
(El) **Dinero** – Money
(El) **Dulce** – Candy
(La) **Escoba** – Broom
(La) **Estrella** – Star
(La) **Fila** – Line
(La) **Foto** – Photo
(La) **Fruta** – Fruit
(El) **Fuego** – Fire
(La) **Fuente** – Fountain

(El) **Gallo** – Rooster
(El) **Hielo** – Ice
(El) **Hogar** – Home
(El) **Hombre Fuerte** – Strongman
(Los) **Jarros** – Jars
(Los) **Juguetes** – Toys
(Los) **Libros** – Books
(La) **Lista** – List
(El) **Lobo** – Wolf
(La) **Lucha libre** – Wrestling
(El) **Luchador** – Wrestler
(La) **Madera** – Wood
(Las) **Manzanas** – Apples
(Las) **Máscaras** – Masks
(El) **Mercado** – Market
(La) **Montaña** – Mountain
(La) **Mosca** – Fly
(La) **Motocicleta** – Motorcycle
(La) **Noche** – Night
(Las) **Naranjas** – Oranges
(El) **Nopal** – Prickly pear
(La) **Olla** – Pot
(La) **Paloma** – Pigeon
(El) **Papel de seda** – Tissue paper
(La) **Pata** – Paw
(El) **Periódico** – Newspaper
(El) **Perro** – Dog

(La) **Piedra** – Rock
(Los) **Pinceles** – Paintbrushes
(La) **Pintura** – Painting
(Las) **Pinzas para la ropa** – Clothespins
(La) **Placita** – Small plaza
(Las) **Plantas** – Plants
(Los) **Plátanos** – Bananas
(El) **Pueblo** – Town
(El) **Puesto** – Booth
(El) **Retrato** – Portrait
(La) **Revista** – Magazine
(El) **Ring de lucha libre** – Wrestling ring
(Las) **Ruedas** – Wheels
(La) **Sandía** – Watermelon
(La) **Silla de montar** – Saddle
(El) **Sol** – Sun
(El) **Sombrero** – Hat
(El) **Techo** – Roof
(El) **Terciopelo** – Velvet
(Las) **Tiendas** – Stores
(Las) **Tijeras** – Scissors
(Los) **Títeres** – Puppets
(El) **Toro** – Bull
(El) **Vaquero** – Cowboy
(Las) **Velas** – Candles
(La) **Ventana** – Window
(La) **Viejita** – Little old lady